THE WINTER KISS OF A ROGUE

THE HOLIDAYS OF THE ARISTOCRACY
BOOK 4

LINDA RAE SANDE

ALSO BY
LINDA RAE SANDE

The Daughters of the Aristocracy

The Kiss of a Viscount

The Grace of a Duke

The Seduction of an Earl

The Sons of the Aristocracy

Tuesday Nights

The Widowed Countess

My Fair Groom

The Sisters of the Aristocracy

The Story of a Baron

The Passion of a Marquess

The Desire of a Lady

The Brothers of the Aristocracy

The Love of a Rake

The Caress of a Commander

The Epiphany of an Explorer

The Widows of the Aristocracy

The Gossip of an Earl

The Enigma of a Widow

The Secrets of a Viscount

The Widowers of the Aristocracy

The Dream of a Duchess

The Vision of a Viscountess

The Conundrum of a Clerk

The Charity of a Viscount

The Cousins of the Aristocracy

The Promise of a Gentleman

The Pride of a Gentleman

The Holidays of the Aristocracy

The Christmas of a Countess

The Knot of a Knight

The Holiday of a Marquess

The Snow Angel of a Duke

The Heirs of the Aristocracy

The Angel of an Astronomer

The Puzzle of a Bastard

The Choice of a Cavalier

The Bargain of a Baroness

The Jewel of an Earl's Heir

The Vixen of a Viscount

The Honor of an Heir

The Rose of a Sultan's Son

The Ladies of the Aristocracy

The Lady of a Grump

The Lady of a Sultan

The Wager of a Wallflower

Beyond the Aristocracy

The Pleasure of a Pirate

The Making of a Mistress

The Bride of a Baronet

The Caton of a Captain

Stella of Akrotiri

Origins

Deminon

Diana

The Lyon's Den (Dragonblade Publishing)

The Courage of a Lyon

The Lady of a Lyon

Note: Translations of select titles are available in German, Italian, Spanish and Portuguese.

CHAPTER 1
A COACH CRASHES

ecember 1815, somewhere in Wiltshire, England

Tossed hard into the side of his traveling coach, Thomas awakened from his slumber with a start. His eyes rounded as his body was thrown toward the ceiling, his breath knocked out of him when his back slammed hard against the unyielding wood. If not for the velvet-covered squabs, he might have suffered more than a twisted arm and a slight cut to his forehead.

The equipage jerked to a halt on its left side, the window pressed against the bottom of a snow-covered ditch. Lumps of coal from the brazier on the floor of the coach scattered about the interior and landed on the curtains of the window. Embers continued to swirl about, leaving trails of orange and red light before they winked out of existence.

Smoke curled up from the puddled curtains. If the fabric caught fire, the thickly varnished wood surrounding the window would soon suffer the same fate.

For the moment he struggled to take a breath, Thomas, Duke of Pendleton, was sure he was experiencing a nightmare.

Is this suppose to be how I die?

The thought had him realizing he needed to move. To inhale deeply while there was still breathable air and make his escape.

Given the position of the coach, he thought to simply stand and push up on the door. There wasn't enough space for him to straighten his body, though, and his hunched posture didn't provide enough leverage for him to force open the door.

The latch refused to budge.

Is this suppose to be how I die?

Near panicked, he lay nearly upside

down on one of the benches and kicked the door latch with a boot heel. The sound of splintering wood was accompanied by the *whoosh* of flames lighting the curtains.

Before he was completely free of the interior, his crushed top hat in one hand and his sprained arm tucked against his midsection, the fire had spread to the squabs.

Backing away from the equipage, his attention went to where his driver should be—and wasn't.

"Fredericks!" he called out, panic nearly closing his throat. Or perhaps it was the cold air.

For a moment, he feared the driver was in the ditch and under the coach, but there was no sign of him. Repeated calls were met only by whinnies of complaint from the two horses still hitched to their yokes.

They were both in the hollow of the ditch, fighting against their awkward-angled hitches. Moving to free them, Thomas struggled with the leather leads. When flames rose from where he had exited the coach, their orange and yellow fingers accenting an already brilliant sunset, the beasts panicked. Despite his attempt to restrain one of them—he was sure he could ride it if necessary—both ran off, their neighs and whinnies loud in the quiet cold.

Cursing, Thomas climbed up to the road and looked both ways. Given the time of year, he wasn't surprised there were no signs of other travelers. There was something near the road about a hundred yards back, though. Something dark against the white snow.

Following the tracks left by the coach, Thomas found Frederick's body at the edge of the road. From his position, it was apparent the driver had fallen from the coach. With no sign of breath coming from the prone man, nor any evidence of a pulse, Thomas realized Fredericks had probably suffered apoplexy.

Is this how he was suppose to die?

Retracing his steps back to the burning coach, Thomas soon understood what had happened.

With their driver having fallen from the

bench, the horses spooked and ran too fast for the road conditions. The coach skidded on the icy surface and careened into the ditch.

A wave of heat from the fire had him stepping back.

Is this how I was supposed to die?

If only he hadn't insisted they continue when they were stopped for a change of horses at the Old Bell at Warminster. The ancient coaching inn wouldn't have had a room for him, though, and although he might have used his title to insist on accommodations, he had no desire to put the owners out of their beds on such a cold night. Not when he was sure Fredericks and the fresh horses could make it to his hunting lodge near Saltford.

Realizing he needed to find shelter or he would freeze to death, Thomas buried his hands into his greatcoat pockets and hurried down the road.

Is this how I'm suppose to die?

He had no idea how far the coach had made it after leaving the Old Bell—he had fallen asleep shortly after they resumed the trip—so he had no sense of how far he was from his hunting lodge.

In the growing gloom of twilight, surely there would be lights on the horizon, especially if he was close to Bath. Or maybe not. The city was built into a depression. Perhaps the lights wouldn't show.

As the cold seemed to penetrate his bones, he thought about why he had decided to go to his hunting lodge in the first place. This time of the year—a fortnight before Christmas—and with this much snow on the ground, it certainly wasn't to hunt. No one would be meeting him there. No servants were scheduled to staff the five-room lodge.

That is where I'm supposed to die.

The thought brought him out of his stupor with a start. No longer sure he was even walking on a road—the white blanket of new-fallen snow under a black canopy created a landscape he had never seen before—he stopped his trudging and slowly turned around in a circle. Surely there must be a light other than the pinpoint diamonds that dotted the sky above. If he hadn't felt so cold, he might have appreciated the Milky Way.

At least he could find the North Star now. He was fairly sure he was heading in a generally northern direction. Earlier, clouds had hid it, as had the falling snow. The accompanying breeze had made travel even more difficult.

As for how far he had come since leaving the coach, he had no idea. He didn't even attempt to pull his chronometer from his waistcoat pocket, for it would require him to remove his gloves, and he would lose what little warmth they were providing.

He slowed his turning, sure he had seen something on the horizon. Squinting, he made out a light in the distance and hurried on, the deepening snow preventing him from jogging as he had been doing when he first left the burning coach.

His thoughts went once again to the poor driver. Fredericks had been with the Pendleton dukedom for half a century. To suffer as he had, his heart probably giving out as he continued to drive the horses, seemed a terrible way to die.

Dying in a burning coach would have been far worse, he supposed. An hour ago, he hadn't welcomed the warmth of the flames. Now he wished he had brought along a piece of the burning coach, or attempted to find one of the coach lanterns. His freezing hands could use the heat, and the lantern would provide some light since the peaches and oranges that had colored the sky only the hour before had given way to an inky blackness that was both infinite and too close for comfort.

Convinced the light on the horizon was growing closer, Thomas picked up the pace, ignoring the gnawing hunger that had begun the hour before. Although he had a scarf wrapped around his neck and most of his clean-shaven face, he was sure his eyelashes sported icicles at their tips.

All at once, the light brightened, dimmed, and brightened again. He slowed his steps. A few more yards and he realized why. The light was coming from beyond a line of perfectly spaced trees.

He nearly collided with a hedgerow encased in a snow blanket, and he followed it until it stopped. From the opening beyond, he paused and stared down a tree-lined lane, the snow-covered branches forming an arch above him that led to several lights.

Lights in windows.

Lots of windows.

Behind his scarf, his face split into a grin of relief.

I'm not going to die on this night.

Given the coverage from the tree branches above, the snow wasn't nearly as deep as on the road. He hurried along the the crushed granite drive, past a fountain covered with a layer of snow, and to the front entrance.

He was sure his pounding on the massive wooden door would wake the dead, but he didn't care.

The house promised warmth, and right now, that's all he wanted.

CHAPTER 2
A LATE NIGHT ARRIVAL
SURPRISES

*M*eanwhile, in the dowager country estate of the Whyte dukedom Katherine settled into her chair at the dining room table and waved to the footman. She felt silly being served dinner here rather than in the smaller breakfast parlor. With son Jonathan's family having departed the day before for London—he and his duchess, Sarah, had decided to spend the Twelve Days at the dukedom's terrace in Mayfair—and her younger son still at university, she no longer had guests to entertain in the house now considered her domain.

Barker poured white wine while Smith-Jones set a bowl of thick soup before her. Although it wasn't as hot as she would have liked, she ate two spoonfuls and directed her attention to her latest book.

The gothic novel wasn't particularly well-written, nor was its premise very original, but the characters were interesting and the action was speeding up to what she thought would be a satisfying climax.

The hero had arrived at his destination, pounding on the door of an abandoned abbey in Yorkshire, his cries for help unheard by anyone. Meanwhile, the heroine was still in the clutches of the kidnapper in a nearby barn while her sister carried a valise filled with money and an ancient relic demanded in the ransom note.

So with the action having moved to the sister, why could Katherine still hear the hero pounding on the door?

She glanced up at hearing a faint yell for help and turned her head in time to see the butler racing past the dining room door.

Her book and soup forgotten, Katherine, Dowager Duchess of Whyte, stood from her chair and made her way to the dining room's entrance. Peeking around the door jamb, she could make out Jackson assisting someone into the vestibule, the visitor's arrival bringing with it a swirl of snowflakes and a blast of cold air she already felt wrapping around her slippered feet.

Curious, she called out, "Jackson, who is it?"

The butler paused in assisting the caller, his look of consternation growing by the moment. "I cannot say, but he's half frozen, Your Grace, and he appears to have been injured."

"Barker!" she called out as she hurried to join the butler, knowing the footman had to be somewhere nearby.

"Here, ma'am," the tall servant replied, appearing from the dining room.

"Start a fire in the front salon. Tell Smith-Jones to bring blankets and find Mrs. Hutchins. It appears as if we'll need bandages," she ordered, unable to hide a wince when she saw their visitor had blood smeared on his face.

The footman nodded in acknowledge-ment and hurried off. Before Katherine had made it into the vestibule, a housemaid was already scurrying into the front salon to see to the fire.

There were no lamps lit in the vestibule, but from the light in the brightly lit hall, Katherine could tell Jackson was seeing to a man of some wealth. Despite the coating of snow on his wool greatcoat, she knew it was of fine quality when Jackson pulled it from the man's body and turned to hang it on a hook. The lining was clearly red satin.

As for the man's top hat, Katherine took it from the shivering man's head and flipped it over to discover a 'Fitzsimmons and Smith' label sewn into the crushed rim.

The hat that makes the gentleman.

Well, this gentleman was freezing. She could hear his teeth chattering from where she was standing—and no wonder. The vestibule was cold. Despite the chilly air, her long-sleeved dinner gown was providing enough warmth for the time being.

Placing the hat on a shelf, she turned

and undid a wet woolen scarf from around his neck. Katherine immediately recognized the trademark scarlet color of Merino wool made by Banks Textiles in Darlington.

The very best wool in all of England.

When her attention went to the man's face, she realized she recognized *him* as well.

"Thomas?" she whispered in awe. She couldn't say more when Smith-Jones appeared with a blanket and some bath linens, and Jackson went to work drying the man's salt-and-pepper hair and ashen face while the footman saw to wrapping the blanket around the man's shoulders.

A streak of blood was left when Jackson pulled the bath linen from his face.

"Oh, dear. He is still bleeding," she said, taking the wet bath linen from Jackson to wipe away the streak in an attempt to locate the source of the blood.

"He has a cut on his forehead, ma'am," Jackson stated.

"Indeed." She turned to discover the

housekeeper, Mrs. Hutchins, armed with an array of bandages and gauze.

"I can see to patchin' 'im up, Your Grace," she said. "Your dinner's gettin' cold."

Katherine caught Barker's attention. "Take him into the front salon and see if he'll drink some brandy." She turned her attention to the butler. "Jackson, we'll need tea and probably some food. Have my dinner brought there."

"Yes, ma'am," the butler replied, hurrying off toward the kitchens.

"Can you walk, Your Grace?"

There was a collective gasp from the footman and the housekeeper. "He's a duke?" Mrs. Hutchins whispered. She immediately dipped a curtsy, although the man didn't see her do it.

His gaze was on Katherine.

And from the expression on his face, it appeared he was regretting his arrival.

CHAPTER 3
A DUKE THAWS
DESPITE A CHILLY
RECEPTION

A few minutes later in the front salon of Whyte Hall Park

Never had brandy tasted as good as the smoky liquid that flowed over his tongue and burned his throat. Never had he drained a glass as quickly as he did in that moment, his hunger nearly as painful as his thawing body.

Nearly as painful as whatever was being done to his forehead. A throbbing had begun somewhere below his hairline and inside his skull. At least his arm no longer ached.

"Careful," Katherine admonished him. "We want you warm. Not drunk." Her gaze lifted to Mrs. Hutchins, who had just finished wrapping the man's head with gauze. She had cleaned and covered the cut with a bandage, clucking about the possible need for stitches.

"Do you think you could eat something?" Katherine asked, ignoring the housekeeper's comments. She held a bowl of thick soup and a spoon, the scent suggesting something fresh from a garden.

His eyes rounding, Thomas was about to reach for the bowl but realized he was still wearing his gloves. His attempt to remove the leather fingers from one hand proved impossible when he couldn't get the fingers of his other hand to work.

Katherine set the bowl on the table next to him and took the chair adjacent to his. "Allow me," she said in a quiet voice. Glancing up at Mrs. Hutchins, who seemed at a loss as to what to do next, she said, "See to our best bedchamber for His Grace. And do include a hot brick or two." She glanced down at his feet. "Send Jackson in. He'll need help removing his boots."

Still shivering, Thomas watched in

fascination as Katherine placed one hand beneath his wrist to lift it while the long fingers of her other hand plucked and pulled each finger of the glove until it came free of his hand. She set it on the table and turned to repeat the process with his other hand.

Thomas saw how his hands shook. Shivered. Practically vibrated. The brief moment when their bare fingers touched, a jolt seemed to awaken the feeling beneath the skin. From the pins and needles sensation that followed, he almost wished his gloves were still on his hands.

"I'll hold the bowl for you," she offered. "Do you think you can handle the spoon?"

Tempted to scold her for treating him like a child, Thomas reached for the utensil and discovered he couldn't grip it. He couldn't make his fingers perform the simple task. "Dammit," he muttered. His eyes once again rounded. "Apologies. I... I—"

"Allow me to help," Katherine said as she lifted the spoon and began feeding him.

"Do you remember what happened? What brought you here?"

He swallowed. "Where exactly are we?"

She furrowed a brunette brow. "Whyte Hall Park, of course. Near Bath," she replied. "How did you get here?"

He swallowed another spoonful of soup. "Walked."

She blinked. "From where?"

Shaking his head, which only worsened the incessant throbbing, he grunted. "Somewhere between here and the Old Bell. The horses were changed there."

"At Warminster?" She said the words with a good deal of shock.

He nodded and winced when the movement caused his headache to worsen.

"That's over twenty miles away," she remarked, feeding him another spoonful of soup. She straightened in her chair. "Did something happen to your traveling coach?"

Resisting the urge to nod, Thomas said, "Fredericks—my driver—he, uh... he seems to have suffered a... apoplexy." He had to swallow the lump that had formed in his throat.

"Oh, dear. Is he... is he still with the coach? I can send my—"

"He is... gone. I... I had to leave him."

Katherine gave a start, as if he'd slapped her across the face, then she appeared flummoxed. "So... why didn't *you* drive the coach? I recall you were at one time rather good at driving coach-and-fours at break-neck speeds near Richmond." The comment held no hint of awe or appreciation of such an accomplishment, but rather derision.

"I was asleep at the time and unaware anything was amiss until I woke up in a coach traveling at breakneck speeds. I nearly broke my neck when it tumbled into a ditch," he countered. "After which it burned up when the curtains caught fire from the coal in the brazier."

Her mouth forming an 'o,' Katherine stared at him a moment before she said, "I thought there was a faint hint of smoke smell about you." She sighed. "Well, it certainly explains why you have that awful gash on your forehead. And why your hat appears as if it was crushed on one side."

Wincing, he took the bowl of soup between his two hands and tilted it to his lips. He drank deeply before setting it aside. "Apologies, but I am starving."

Katherine angled her head to one side. "I take it you didn't eat at the Old Bell?"

He shook his head. "I would have spent the night there, but—"

"No room at the inn," she finished for him. "Not this time of the year." She reached for the bottle of brandy and refilled his glass.

Not trusting his fingers, he took it between the palms of his hands. "This is the best brandy I have ever drunk," he stated.

"It's the same brand of brandy you drank when you were driving coach-and-fours at breakneck speeds," she said in a tone filled with rebuke. Her brows suddenly furrowed. "Were you on your way to Saltford? To your hunting lodge?"

He set aside the glass of brandy. "How do you know about that?"

She gave him a quelling glance. "We

were once betrothed, or have you forgotten?"

The pained expression on his face only worsened. "I had hoped *you* had," he whispered, glad the housekeeper had left the room.

She shoved another spoonful of soup into his mouth. "A woman never forgets being left at the altar."

Thomas swallowed and then let out an audible sigh. "I suppose not," he agreed.

She dropped her head to one side. "You never did tell me why." When he didn't immediately respond, she added, "When you didn't so much as send a note, I worried you had broken your neck whilst driving a coach-and-four at breakneck speeds."

"You couldn't have missed me too much," he accused, sounding angrier than he felt.

Jerking at hearing the sound of rebuke in *his* voice, Katherine scoffed. "What's *that* supposed to mean?"

"You married Whyte."

"Well, not because I wanted to," she

countered, trying hard to keep her voice low. Jackson would appear at any moment to help with his boots, and she didn't want the servant learning their ancient history. "At least, not at the time."

"Less than a fortnight later, I heard."

Katherine swallowed, deciding not to mention it had only been a week. "It was a quick arrangement," she acknowledged.

"You couldn't have waited for me?"

Blinking, she regarded him with disbelief. "How long was it before you finally made an appearance in London again?"

His eyes briefly darted to the ceiling as he contemplated his answer. "Four... mayhap five months."

She simply stared at him, as if the answer to his question should have been obvious. "Where *were* you?"

He dipped his head. "On the Continent."

Her eyes narrowed. "During the French Revolution? Whatever in the world—?"

"I worked for Chamberlain," he stated, referring to the viscount who headed the Foreign Office. When she didn't seem to comprehend his meaning, he added, "As a spy." He paused a moment, not surprised at seeing her look of shock. "Chamberlin knew there would be a number of players looking to fill the void left when the king and so many aristocrats lost their heads. He wanted to be sure..." He rolled his eyes and sighed. "We hoped it would be someone favorable to Great Britain. Even tried to make it so, but..."

"Instead it was Bonaparte."

"Exactly," he said at the same moment Jackson appeared. The butler carried Katherine's abandoned dinner on a tray, silver domes covering two plates, and set it on the table next to her chair.

"I had Cook dish up a dinner for His Grace," Jackson said in a quiet voice.

"Thank you for thinking of me," Thomas said, straightening.

Katherine experienced a moment of embarrassment at having forgotten the duke's hunger. "His Grace requires assistance with removing his boots. If his feet are as frozen as his fingers were..." She didn't finished the sentence, realizing

Thomas might have suffered frostbite or worse.

"Of course, my lady. Your Grace," Jackson said as he knelt and worked to remove the boots. "I took the liberty of finding a pair of stockings for you, sir."

"Much appreciated," Thomas replied. "I'm afraid I didn't think to grab my valise when I left the coach. It's probably burned in the fire." He winced several times as the butler struggled with his Hobys, clenching his teeth in an effort to keep from cursing.

"There are still some of Whyte's clothes up in the master bedchamber dressing room," Katherine said. "You're welcome to take whatever will fit you."

"Much appreciated," he murmured, not bothering to hide his expression of pain.

It was Katherine's turn to wince between bites of roast beef and gravy when Jackson finally managed to free the duke's feet from the boots and the two pairs of woolen stockings he wore. "Could you bring a tub of warm water so he can soak his feet?"

"Right away, ma'am."

Jackson hurried out of the room as Thomas finally let out a curse of frustration. He was attempting to wiggle his toes, but the sensation of pins and needles was almost too much to bear.

"Would you like some dinner?" she asked, holding out the plate Jackson had delivered.

"I thought you were never going to ask," he replied, taking the fork and plate from her.

Katherine gave him a look of surprise when he was able to hold both. "I see your fingers have recovered."

He grimaced. "My hands, yes."

"What's wrong?"

"I may have frostbite," he whispered. "I can't feel my feet."

Setting aside her fork, Katherine knelt before him and took one of his bare feet between her hands.

"Tickling me is not going to help," he warned.

She gave him a quelling glance as she began to rub his skin. Her hands were warm against his chilled flesh, and after a few minutes of discomfort, he began to appreciate what she was doing.

"Careful, or I'm going to want you to do that more often."

Lifting the other foot, she repeated her ministrations as he groaned and hissed and took exaggerated breaths. "You sound like you're trying to give birth," she accused.

He chuckled, the first hint of humor he had displayed the entire evening. "You probably didn't make a sound when Whyte's whelps were born, did you?"

Katherine scoffed. "I might be a duchess, but that did not prevent me from screaming and yelling and cursing at the top of my lungs," she countered. "I suppose you weren't even at home when your duchess gave birth to your heir."

His eyes rounded at the implied insult. "I was, too," he claimed. "I wasn't allowed upstairs, though. Paced in my study for what seemed like hours."

"Probably because it was."

"For both of them," he murmured. "I have two sons." He sobered and swallowed hard.

Giving up her hold on his foot, she sat back on her heels and regarded him with a sad expression. "Do you miss her? Lydia was the perfect choice for you," she said in a quiet voice. The Duchess of Pendleton had died of a fever in 1812, the cause of which hadn't been determined.

Thomas took a deep breath. "I did. For awhile. I liked her. Very much," he murmured. "I don't think she liked me as much, though."

Katherine scoffed. "She loved you, you idiot," she stated, hiding her annoyance when Jackson reappeared with a tub of water while Barker followed with bath linens. She managed to stand with the duke's help, surprised at the strength he displayed in doing so.

Unwilling to carry on the conversation with the servants present, Thomas sat back and placed his feet in the warm water. "This is perfect. I won't require your services the rest of the night."

Jackson's gaze darted to his mistress. "Your Grace?"

"What bedchamber did Mrs. Hutchins prepare for His Grace?"

"The master bedchamber, ma'am. There's a good fire going in there now, and hot bricks at the end of the bed."

Katherine resisted the urge to question the choice. She had requested Thomas be given the best bedchamber, though, and she supposed it was the finest in the house. "Very good. I'll escort His Grace there when he's ready to retire."

"Will His Grace require assistance climbing the stairs?"

Thomas shook his head. "If I can't walk, I'll simply sleep in this chair," he muttered.

"Very good, Your Grace." Jackson turned his attention on his mistress. "Your Grace?"

"In the morning, have Mr. Thompson and Barker head south in search of the duke's coach driver, and anything else they might find from the coach," Katherine ordered, glancing at the footman to see how he might react. She was surprised to see him display excitement, as if he was glad to carry out the duty. Or perhaps he merely wanted an excuse to leave the house. "The horses might be there," she added, remembering Thomas had said he had unhitched them.

"I'll have them leave at first light, ma'am," Jackson replied. "Good night."

She watched her servants take their leave and turned her attention to her dinner plate.

"Why didn't you wait for me?" Thomas asked, his gaze on the flames in the fireplace.

"What?"

"Why did you marry Whyte?"

Setting aside her plate, Katherine took a deep breath and let it out slowly. "My parents wouldn't have survived the scandal if I hadn't married when I did," she claimed.

He jerked his head to regard her with furrowed brows. "Scandal?" he repeated. "What scandal?"

She stared at him for some time before she whispered. "I was with child."

Thomas blinked. "You were *pregnant*?" He straightened. "When *we* were to be married?"

Her expression didn't change, and she didn't respond.

His eyes widened. "*I* took your virtue. I was the only one..." He stopped speaking and cursed softly.

"Indeed," she said in a quiet voice. "Jonathan, the current Duke of Whyte, is your son."

CHAPTER 4
TRUTH HELPS TO
WARM A HEART

Katherine did her best to keep her head held up as Thomas regarded her with an expression that changed from shock to disbelief to horror and finally realization.

"Whyte's whelp was mine?" he whispered.

"*Is* yours," she stated, "and please don't refer to him as a whelp. He's a duke now."

Thomas gave a start. "Jonathan? He's really *my* son?" He swallowed. "Who... who else knows?"

Turning to be sure no servants were hovering near the door, Katherine said, "No one, of course. Not even my lady's maid."

Thomas shook his head. "Surely Whyte—"

"He did not," she interrupted. "I didn't even tell him I was with child until he mentioned I looked as if I was eating too many cakes at tea time. That was several months after we wed. And then, when I told him why my belly was rounding, he was so... so *thrilled*." She said the last word in a quieter voice as her gaze turned on her mind's eye. "That was the first time he ever told me he loved me."

Wincing, Thomas remarked, "He always held a candle for you. Even when we were at university, he spoke of courting you. I think our betrothal hurt him."

"Oh, I know it did," she admitted. "I took advantage of it. When he paid a call two days after we were to marry, he proposed. I was desperate, and I hadn't heard from you, so of course I accepted." She sighed. "In doing so, I didn't consider if it would hurt you or not because—"

"You hated me."

"I didn't *hate* you," she countered. "But I was hurt and confused. I hadn't heard from you—no one had—and being with child certainly didn't help."

Wincing, Thomas sat in silence for a moment. "I recall him crowing about getting a child on you. We were at Brooks's," he remarked. "I don't think I was ever as angry as I was at that moment."

Katherine gave a start. "You didn't—?"

"I didn't say a word. I didn't even throw a punch," he said as he shook his head.

"But you hated me," she guessed, not making it a question.

He shook his head. "No. I hated the frogs for deciding to stage a revolt at the worst possible time in my career as a spy," he muttered. "And I hated Chamberlain for sending me."

Katherine swallowed as she stared at him. "Why did you go? Couldn't you have... begged off? Surely Chamberlain knew you were to marry..." She broke off, her mouth rounding in an 'o.'

"What is it?" he asked, leaning forward in his chair.

"Chamberlain knew," she murmured. "I know Mother had an invitation delivered to Fitzsimmons Manor—she was friends with his wife, Caroline—and yet he sent you to France anyway," she whispered. Her face took on a look of anger. "For a reason."

Thomas straightened. "What are you talking about?"

She inhaled softly. "Spite. My father and Chamberlain did not get along. Not in the least."

"I do recall there was a bit of frost there," Thomas agreed.

"Father always voted against funding the Foreign Office. He was an opponent of the merger of the Northern and Southern Departments. Talked about it at every dinner party he hosted. He did not like change," she stated on a sigh. "So Chamberlain deprived me of you to embarrass my father."

Thomas dipped his head. "And didn't consider what it would do to us," he whispered.

She winced but nodded. "I take it you no longer work for the Foreign Office?" she asked. "I hear the pay is terrible."

"Pay?" he repeated, scoffing. "What

pay?" Rolling his eyes, he leaned back and closed his eyes. "I left the service when Father died. Probably should have well before then. Took me months to learn how to be a duke," he explained. "Thank the gods he had a decent man of business and a couple of good foremen overseeing the farms, or I fear the dukedom would have gone back to the Crown."

"And now?" she prompted.

He gave a start. "I admit I liked the position. I liked having influence—"

"Power," she interrupted, curious as to why he spoke as if he was no longer the duke.

"The wealth and the privilege it afforded me—"

"Political leverage," she said in a whisper.

"The means to help my tenant farmers..." When Katherine didn't interrupt, he glanced over at her.

"I'm not sure Whyte was always very good about that," she murmured, "but Jonathan..." She inhaled softly. "Jonathan is."

Thomas stared at her as he swallowed.

"I... I met him. When he took his seat in the House of Lords." He furrowed a brow. "He doesn't bear much of a resemblance to Whyte, but I didn't give it a thought."

She shrugged. "I don't think anyone did, since they both had dark hair and similar jawlines," she said, a wan smile appearing. "And James, my other son, is of a similar appearance."

"Do you think Jonathan resembles me?"

She regarded him a moment as she angled her head to one side. "He has your eyes," she said softly.

Thomas dipped his head. "Do you think there will ever be a time we can tell him the truth?"

Katherine winced. "I doubt it."

"Would it be all right if I... if I made friends with him?"

She gave him a watery grin. "I certainly wouldn't object." Noticing how weary he had become, she added, "But let's talk more about it on the morrow. We need to get you upstairs and into a warm bed."

"Will you be in it, too?" he asked, lifting

his feet from the tub to place them on the bath linens.

"For warmth? Or for something more?" she asked, suspicious.

His gaze darted to the side. "Can't it be for both?" He pulled on the stockings Jackson had left for him on the hearth, sighing as their warmth enveloped his feet.

Katherine gave him a grin. "Why don't we start with warmth?" she suggested. She stood and helped him to stand before the two slowly made their way up the stairs.

CHAPTER 5
EVERYTHING THAT'S CHANGED REMAINS THE SAME

half hour later Katherine regarded her reflection in her dressing table mirror and winced. The green dinner gown she wore was not a good color against her skin, nor was the severe hairstyle her lady's maid had done earlier that morning. What must Thomas have thought as they sat and conversed in the front salon?

"Is that man goin' to be all right?" Johnson asked as she removed the pins from her mistress' hair. "I heard he was nearly frozen to death."

"That man is His Grace, the Duke of Pendleton, and yes, it appears he will be fine," Katherine replied. "There's a possibility his feet suffered frostbite, though. We'll know more in the morning."

Johnson inhaled softly. "Is it true his coach burned up?"

Katherine furrowed her brows as she undid the clasp of an emerald necklace and collected the gold and gemstone jewelry into one hand. The piece was part of a parure Whyte had gifted her on the day of their tenth wedding anniversary. The matching bracelet was still on her wrist.

"Unfortunately, it is." Although she was annoyed word had already spread regarding their guest's situation, she couldn't chastise her servants. Given the weather, they hadn't been to town for several days. A lack of gossip coupled with the impending holiday—there was nothing they could do for the hanging of the greens until Christmas Eve—had them edgier than usual.

"His driver, Fredericks, apparently suffered some sort of heart ailment and fell from the coach. The horses were spooked and ran. Poor man ended up in the snow somewhere," she explained. "I've instructed Jackson to have Mr. Thompson head out in the morning to search," she added, referring to the groom who acted as her driver when she was in residence at Whyte Hall Park. "Barker is going along to help. Apparently, the coach ended up in a ditch."

"A ditch?" the lady's maid repeated. "But the nearest ditch is miles from here," she murmured.

"At least five, I think," Katherine agreed. "That's how far His Grace had to walk to reach the house. It's no wonder he was so frozen when he arrived."

From the servant's reflection in the mirror, Katherine knew Johnson was as impressed as she was horrified by what had happened. "I expect our guest will sleep later than usual, and given the hour—goodness, is it already past one?—I expect I will want to as well," she said. "Don't bother to come up until I ring for you."

"Very good, ma'am." Johnson brushed out Katherine's long, brunette hair. "Since it's such a cold night, I've pulled out your thickest night rail and a pair of stockings."

Managing to keep her expression from showing distaste—her warmest night rail was also her ugliest—Katherine merely nodded. "Very good. Do go to bed. I can finish up here," she said.

Johnson dipped a curtsy. "Your Grace." She hurried out the door, making sure the latch clicked when it closed.

Refolding the night rail Johnson had left on the end of the bed, Katherine put it away and found a different one in her bureau. Although it wasn't as fancy as a French gown might have been, it did feature a lower cut bodice and delicate lace trim around the neckline and the end of the long sleeves.

For a moment, she almost had herself talked out of joining Thomas. The twenty-five years that had passed since their last time sharing a bed hadn't been kind. Although her once pert breasts were fuller, they had also succumbed to gravity. Her hips were wider due to birthing two baby boys, and lines radiated from the corners of her eyes.

At least her hair was still dark. Only a

few stray grays interrupted the rich chocolate brown that fell well past her shoulders.

She had a thought to remove the silk stockings she had worn all day and decided against it. They provided a modicum of warmth and hid the bare skin of her calves and knees.

Blowing out two of the candle lamps, she helped herself to the third and made her way through the dressing room to the door of the master bedchamber. She knocked twice before turning the handle and daring a peek into the room. From the higher temperature, she knew a servant had set a blazing fire in the fireplace.

"I was beginning to think you had changed your mind," Thomas remarked. He was on the bed, the blankets and linens covering him pulled up nearly to his neck, and his eyes were closed.

"I didn't," Katherine replied, setting the candle lamp on the nightstand. She went about turning down the other lamps in the room, the dark blue and green furnishings appearing almost black in the resulting gloom. "But I did have to allow my lady's maid to undo my hair and undress me."

He opened one eye. "I could have done that."

Chuckling, she stood next to the bed. "Do you have a preference for which side you'd like me to take?"

"On top of me, of course."

"Bounder."

Although his eyes were closed, he said, "You know when you stand in front of the fire like that, I can see right through whatever it is you're wearing."

"Oh, dear," she replied, making quick work of lifting the blankets and sliding in between the bed linens. "Then it's best you keep your eyes closed."

He grunted. "Why? You're still gorgeous." Before she had a chance to settle in completely, he had a bare arm behind her shoulders. He pulled her so she was half atop him. Her head landed in the small of his shoulder, one arm lay draped over his bare chest, and a leg ended up resting between his. "And I always adored holding you like this," he added on a sigh.

Katherine gave a start, realizing she had settled against him the same way she had all those years ago, as if a quarter of a century hadn't passed. "I always adored the way you held me." She inhaled deeply, the familiar scents of citrus, spice, and musk filling her nostrils. "You even smell the same."

"That's because I still buy my cologne at Floris," he muttered.

"I cannot believe you're not sound asleep," she whispered, now well aware he wore nothing in the way of a nightshirt or drawers. Although his manhood wasn't completely erect, she could feel its length pressed against her hip.

"I cannot believe I'm about to embarrass myself by falling asleep," he countered. He turned his head to kiss the top of hers. "I promise I shall do better when I awaken."

She grinned. "I promise to let you."

A moment later, and they were both sound asleep.

CHAPTER 6
THE THROES OF
PASSION

*S*ometime in the middle of the night
Sure he wasn't alone and sure he wasn't in his own bed, Thomas struggled to sit up.

The movement was made more difficult due to the feminine body that was keeping his right side warm. The heat he felt on his left side was due to the dying fire in a fireplace he didn't recognize.

"Are you all right?"

The whispered query had him opening his eyes wider and turning his head to discover a familiar face staring at him with worry.

"Where am I?"

She inhaled softly. "In the master bedchamber of Whyte Hall Park. Near Bath. You arrived last evening—"

"Frozen," he finished for her, the events of the day before coming back to him in a flash. "Apologies. I was having a terrible dream." He scrubbed a hand over his face as if to wipe away the nightmare.

"I don't doubt it," she replied. "Your heart has been racing for a few minutes. Enough to wake me."

"I'm sorry."

"Don't be. I merely thought you were…" She allowed the sentence to trail off as she touched her lips to his chest and kissed it. The hand that rested on his stomach drifted down to the nest of dark curls from which his manhood stood at attention. "Aroused."

He inhaled sharply. "Seems I am. I haven't slept with a woman in… well, in a very long time," he stammered.

She lifted her body onto an elbow and rested her head in her hand. "It's been some time for me. Whyte was the only man…" Clamping her mouth shut, Katherine regarded Thomas with an expression of regret. "I'm sorry. I didn't mean to mention him."

He gave a start. "I don't mind," he replied. "Well, I would if you accidentally said his name whilst we were in the throes of passion," he amended.

"The throes of passion?" she repeated, a grin lighting her face in the dim light.

"I know it's been a long time—for the both of us—but... I wish to make love to you."

Katherine lowered her gaze to his shoulder. "Because I'm the one you've discovered sleeping with you, or...?"

"I will admit proximity has a good deal to do with it, but even if you had slept in your own bed, I think I could have found you," he claimed. He lifted his head and turned to kiss her on the lips, which had her eyes rounding in surprise. "I would have kissed you awake and had my way with you."

Grinning, she said, "And now?"

"Well, you're already awake."

"I can pretend I'm not," she said, rolling onto her back and closing her eyes.

His deep chuckle had the bed vibrating even as the covers were suddenly gone from atop her body.

"Oh!" she cried out in a whisper. She tittered as he climbed over her and captured her lips with his. The kiss was soft at first. Soft and tentative. A means to part her lips so his tongue could invade her mouth and explore her teeth. Taste the tea and brandy they had drunk. The meal they had shared in the small salon.

When he pulled away, he stared down at her and swallowed. His gaze drifted to her bare shoulders and arms and then down to her breasts where they mounded and pressed into his chest. "I distinctly remember you were wearing a night rail," he whispered.

Her eyes darted to the side. "I might have had to remove it some time ago. I don't know if you're aware or not, but you're rather hot when you're sleeping. I almost feared you had a fever."

Thomas furrowed a brow. "Perhaps I do," he replied, his lips descending so they touched and traced her collar bone. His entire body lifted from hers and moved down a few inches, and his lips followed suit until he had one of her nipples between them.

Inhaling sharply, Katherine lifted her chest and whispered a series of 'yes's.

Giving up his hold on one nipple, he moved to the other. Before capturing it with his teeth and tongue, he murmured, "You were always so positive."

"I can't imagine saying 'no,'" she countered, her hands sliding down the sides of his torso.

He suckled her nipple for a moment before moving farther down her body with his lips, kissing here and there as he went.

"Where ever are you going?" she managed to get out between gasps for air.

Chuckling, he said, "If I tell you, you'll start saying 'no,' and I will not listen." His hands moved to beneath her knees and lifted them so they were draped over his shoulders.

Katherine inhaled sharply. Inhaled again

when his tongue invaded her most private place. "Thomas," she managed to whisper, exhaling sharply. "No!"

His hands sliding beneath the globes of her bottom, he plundered her womanhood with his tongue, circling and suckling and kissing until her soft 'yes's replaced a few 'no's. When he thrust his tongue inside her, she let out a soft cry as her body shuddered and shook beneath his hold.

A moment later, and he was atop her, his engorged manhood thrusting into her, his movements matching those of her body as her insides pulled him in deeper and deeper with each wave of her pleasure.

He intended to make it last far longer than it did. He intended to slow his movements, make her beg, coax a few more 'yes's out of her before he allowed his release.

Alas, it was not to be, for her cresting waves had him succumbing to a climax he hadn't experienced in a very long time.

He lifted his head and allowed the intense spasm of pleasure to have its way with him. To force his body to seize and his manhood to finally release its seed into her.

Suspended over her for what seemed like several minutes, euphoria sweeping over him in an all-consuming sensation, he finally relaxed and lowered his body to hers.

Katherine wrapped her arms around his back and hung on, as if she didn't trust him to remain right where he was.

"Oh, now I'm quite sure you have a fever," she whispered, her voice filled with a combination of awe and worry.

Thomas covered one of her breasts with his mouth and stifled a chuckle. When he came up for air, he said, "Fever or not, we're doing this again," he whispered. "I'll not take no for an answer."

She blinked. "I would never say no," she claimed.

Even as he continued to chuckle, he rolled off her body and fell asleep on his side.

Sighing softly, Katherine pulled the bed linens over them both and wondered how he could sleep when her entire body seemed alive for the first time in a very long time.

CHAPTER 7
A PLAN WITH NO FUTURE

*N*ear dawn

"Can you stay?" Katherine asked, rather liking how Thomas had linked his fingers with hers beneath the covers.

"Is that an invitation?"

She inhaled softly. "Yes. Or... did you have plans to spend Christmas with your sons?"

He shook his head. "No plans."

She blinked. "You said you were on your way to your hunting lodge."

It was his turn to blink. "I did?"

Trying to remember exactly what he had said the night before, Katherine inhaled suddenly. "I asked if you were on your way to Saltford. You... you asked how I knew about your hunting lodge."

Thomas winced and rolled onto his back. "I was on my way," he admitted.

Katherine gave a start. "Oh, dear. Your servants are probably expecting you. They no doubt wonder what's become of you. I can have my driver head there after he sees to your driver. Let them know—"

"There's no need," he interrupted, squeezing her fingers.

"What?"

"There aren't any servants at the hunting lodge."

Furrowing her brows, she angled her head to better see him. "Not even a cook?"

He shook his head in the pillow.

"Were you going to cook for yourself? I mean, I can imagine you knowing how to boil water, but—"

"I wasn't going to cook for myself."

She inhaled softly. "There aren't exactly any coaching inns or... or pubs very close to your lodge," she countered. "What did you expect to eat?"

He audibly sighed. "I didn't plan to eat anything."

Scoffing, she lifted herself onto an elbow and stared down at him. "What? Were you planning to starve?"

A grimace marred his features. "As a matter of fact, yes."

"To death?" she asked in disbelief.

"Actually, I thought I might drink myself into a stupor and not wake up."

For a moment, Katherine thought he might be teasing her, but the serious expression on his face convinced her he was telling the truth. She remembered how he had referred to being a duke in the past tense the night before, as if he was no longer. "If you truly wished to die, you could have done so last night. When the coach burned," she accused. "You said you had to escape," she added, her voice sounding with hope.

"The thought of dying in a fire held little appeal," he replied, immediately understanding her comment. There had been that awful moment when the coach careened into the ditch. A moment when his life seemed to flash before his eyes, and there was one thought that stuck in his mind when the equipage came to a halt and the smoke started to fill the interior.

Is this really how I want to die?

"So... you could have simply fallen into the snow and frozen to death," she countered.

He stared at her. "Freezing to death would have been nearly as bad as burning to death," he reasoned, remembering how numbness had changed to the painful sensation of pins and needles he had felt in his extremities. How his eyelashes threatened to freeze together so he might be unable to blink or open his eyes completely. How easy it would have been to simply keep his eyes closed and slowly fall into oblivion.

Is this really how I want to die?

"So... instead, you walked miles and miles and nearly froze to death looking for a light."

He nodded in the pillow.

Tears pricked the corners of her eyes.

"Oh, Thomas. Why ever did you wish to die in the first place?"

His gaze darted to the door, as if he wished they might be interrupted by a servant. He knew the housemaids were up and about, probably rushing around due to his presence in the house. "I am fifty years old," he stated in a hoarse whisper.

Giving her head a shake, she said, "And I am five-and-forty..."

"*You* have something to live for."

The words hung in the air for a long time before she said, "Don't you?"

Swallowing hard, he stared at her. "Do I?"

She winced. "You have three sons," she stated, including her firstborn in the count.

It was his turn to wince. "My oldest, John... he's been seeing to the ducal properties these past few years. He's far more efficient at managing the estates than I ever was. He'll make an excellent addition to Parliament."

"And your youngest?" she prompted.

"George returned from his Grand Tour last month. Wants to take up archaeology with some viscount in the Kingdom of the Two Sicilies."

Katherine furrowed a brow. "Viscount Henley, perhaps?" she guessed. She had never met the man, but accounts of his Ancient Greek and Roman discoveries were frequently documented in *The Times*.

"Yes, that's him."

"He's mentored a number of young men interested in the avocation," she remarked. "From what I heard when I was last in London, he's very good."

"George said the same. Once he leaves, I doubt I'll ever see him again."

She furrowed both brows and angled her head to one side. "And then there's Jonathan."

He gave a start. "I had no reason to suspect Jonathan was my son," he whispered.

"He's married now. You have an adorable grandchild."

He lifted himself onto an elbow. "I do?"

Grinning, she nodded. "Jonathan's duchess bore him a son only six months ago. He is still a babe, but John has a set of lungs on him that can wake the dead," she claimed, once again wincing. "So you see, you have no excuse to die before your time."

He relaxed back onto the bed and stared up at the ceiling. Until that moment, he hadn't noticed the ornate plasterwork or the stucco cherubs decorating each corner, their expressions conveying mischief and mayhem. "My father died well before he was fifty."

"Your father was a crotchety old fart," she replied with a sniff.

Thomas burst out laughing, which had Katherine grinning even as a blush colored her face.

"He was that," Thomas murmured in agreement. He took a deep breath and let it out. "What about you?"

Her eyes widened. "What about me? Do you think I'm a crotchety old fart now that I've five-and forty?" Realizing her entire front was uncovered, she quickly pulled the bed linens up and gripped them to her chest.

He scoffed, obviously disappointed she

hid her bare breasts from his view. He'd had plans for them, but the conversation had veered into subjects not conducive to making love. "Hardly. Is that what you think of me? Now that you know I'm fifty?"

She shook her head. "Never," she whispered. Her attention darted to his midsection. "Especially after you shocked me last night."

He gave a start. "How did I manage that?"

Giving him a quelling glance, she stuck out her tongue and pulled it back into her mouth.

He chuckled. "Ah, yes. I learned some tricks since we last made love all those years ago," he admitted. "I was hoping to use them again. On you," he added in a whisper.

"Oh? Does that mean... does that mean you're staying?"

"Is that an invitation?"

She nodded. "For as long as you'd like."

Thomas considered her words for a few moments before he said, "That could be several years," he warned. "Now that I have so much to live for."

"Several years means we may become a scandal," she reasoned, her eyes widening with mirth.

"Not if we finally get married," he countered.

She gave a start. "Are you proposing?"

He scoffed. "I already did. Twenty-five years ago."

Giggling, Katherine lowered herself until she leaned over his chest and kissed him. "Well, I'm not letting you get away this time," she warned.

He returned the kiss and soon had her flat on her back, her gasps and titters urging him to continue what he had started earlier that morning.

If he was going to die, he was going to do so while he was buried inside her, experiencing an earth-shattering orgasm.

And not a moment before.

CHAPTER 8
A MORNING FILLED
WITH PROMISE

wo hours later

Katherine awoke with a start, sure someone was watching her. She lifted her head, expecting to see her lady's maid fussing with a selection of day gowns.

But the only other person in the bedchamber was Thomas, and he was regarding her with a wan grin. He was still under the covers, his head half-hidden by his pillow. "Morning, sleepy head," he said before touching his lips to her forehead.

"Good morning, handsome," she replied, one hand going to his forehead. Her brows furrowed as she flattened her palm over the area that wasn't covered by the bandage. "You feel feverish," she murmured.

"Ah, but I am. Feverishly in need of you," he replied with a grin.

Torn between admonishing him and kissing him, she decided on disbelief. "Really? I must look a sight," she remarked, lifting herself onto an elbow. A curtain of her dark hair fell onto the arm he had wrapped beneath her breasts.

"Oh, you are. A sight for sore eyes and then some," he murmured, his lips covering one of her nipples.

She didn't bother pulling away. Not when it meant giving up an opportunity to experience a few more minutes of pleasure with the duke with whom she had at one time expected to live her entire life.

Although she had pretended innocence and shock when he had first made love to her all those years ago, during an afternoon when he was allowed to take her for a ride on his high-perch phaeton in Rotten Row, she had secretly wished for a different sort of ride.

And he had provided it.

His possession of a terrace so close to Hyde Park meant they could ride in public and then hurry off to spend an hour in his bedchamber, him teaching her what to do for him while he seemed to already know what to do for her.

His carnal attentions had been shocking at first. Shocking but so welcome. Soon, the two were spending nearly every afternoon at his terrace, making love and sharing secrets. Making plans and sharing stories. Making merry and sharing gossip.

Right up until the day before their wedding.

When his hand waved in front of her face, Katherine gave a start. "Where were you?" he asked.

She glanced down, stunned to discover he was already atop her. Her legs were wrapped around his thighs, and her core throbbed with need of him. "I was remembering what you used to do to me after our rides in the park."

"Fondly, I hope," he responded, his manhood nudging at her entrance.

Inhaling sharply, she nodded in the

pillow. "Always." She lifted her hips, which had his cock entering her halfway.

Stunned at her move, Thomas chuckled as he pushed into her all the way. "I rather enjoyed teaching you how to make love. Now I'm hoping I don't embarrass myself."

"Why do you think you would?" she asked, once again lifting her hips in an attempt to make him begin the familiar thrusting she had come to appreciate.

"I haven't bedded a woman in a long time, let alone three times in less than a day."

She grinned when he finally pulled out and thrust into her. "After nearly freezing to death, no less," she whispered.

"I thought to take it slow this morning," he said quietly. He kissed her engorged nipples. "But—"

"Hurry," she breathed.

He nodded, unable to form words to respond. He was already caught up in the maelstrom of what was about to happen, every one of his frantic thrust met by hers.

Neither lasted long, their pleasures cresting and crashing at the same time.

Thomas remained suspended above her for a long time before he gave into his sudden exhaustion, his eyes locked with hers.

Katherine guided his body down until his head rested on her pillow. Wrapping her arms around his back as far as she could, she held on, preventing him from rolling off of her. "Stay. Stay here with me," she begged in a whisper.

"I'm not going anywhere," he replied, his voice faraway.

Finally relaxing into the bed, she let out a long sigh. Moving a hand to the back of his head, she speared her fingers through his graying hair until she felt him shiver.

"When you said that, did you mean... for a moment?" he asked. "Or... or longer?"

"Both," Katherine replied, remembering what he had said about the hunting lodge. She wasn't about to allow him to leave Whyte Hall Park if he intended to die.

"What if you... what if you grow tired of me?"

She turned her head so she faced him,

their noses nearly touching. "Do you think you can manage bedding me twice a week?"

"I can imagine far more than that," he replied. His brows furrowed, as if he realized he might be overconfident in his estimation. "As for if I can actually manage it, I would say at least three times, I should think."

She tittered. "Then you're stuck here with me. Except for a few weeks every year when we'll go to Bath to attend some entertainments."

"You make it sound so awful," he accused.

"Can you manage it?" she repeated, a look of worry crossing her face.

He scoffed. "The more important question is, can you?" Grinning, he asked, "You haven't changed your mind about marrying me?"

Katherine blinked, just then remembering their conversation at dawn. "Will you show up for the ceremony?"

For a moment, he looked hurt. "I promise I will," he said. "Unless I'm dead from all this lovemaking," he amended.

Noise beyond the window had them both sitting up. Katherine inhaled softly. "They're back," she murmured.

"Who?"

She stepped out of the bed and lifted her dressing robe from the floor. "A footman and my driver. They left this morning right after dawn. Took the traveling coach to go look for your driver," she explained, settling the garment over her shoulders and wrapping it around her body. Moving to the window, she pulled back the drape on one side and peered out the frost-rimmed glass. "They're pulling two horses."

Thomas joined her, his naked body pressed to her back as he peeked over her shoulder. "The nags must have returned to the coach after the fire died down," he reasoned. "I intended to ride one of them after I unhitched them, but they ran off." He wrapped his arms around her body. "I suppose I should go down."

She turned her head and rested her chin on her shoulder. "Not like that, you're not," she said.

He chuckled. "Ring for your maid,

sweeting," he suggested. "I fear it's time for me to face the day."

Knowing he was referring to the fate of his driver, Katherine stepped away from the window and kissed him. "We'll do it together," she said. Backing away from him, she arched a brow. "For a man who claims to be fifty, you don't look a day over five-and-forty."

Chuckling, Thomas inhaled deeply. "I suddenly feel far younger, if you must know."

"Good," she replied, understanding his comment. Despite what faced them downstairs, she felt more alive than she had in a very long time. "I'll ring for my maid and have hot water brought up for the both of us." She disappeared through the dressing room door, well aware Thomas watched her exit.

She made sure to give her hips an extra sway as she did so.

"You're killing me," he accused in a hoarse whisper.

CHAPTER 9
A MIRACLE REVEALED

a half-hour later Johnson helped Katherine from the copper bathtub, the water still warm. "You seem in a hurry this morning, ma'am."

"That's because I am," the duchess replied, wrapping herself in the large bath linen. "We have a guest, and I saw the servants returning this morning from their errand."

She had been disappointed to discover her lady's maid knew nothing of the details. She had rung for Johnson before the driver had pulled into the stable behind the house. "I saw they rescued the horses from the duke's traveling coach." She took a seat at the dressing table, amazed at seeing her reflection in the mirror.

Despite the late night and little sleep she had managed between bouts of lovemaking, she appeared as if she had youthened by a decade.

"Such a tragedy," Johnson said as she brushed out her mistress' hair. "I do hope they found His Grace's driver."

"Indeed. His Grace feels awful about what happened to him." She watched as Johnson quickly wrapped her hair into a chignon and pinned it into place. "I've invited the duke to stay..." She almost said 'forever' but caught herself. "For Christmas and the Twelve Days."

"He doesn't have a family?"

Katherine winced. She had a family, and yet they had returned to London to spend Christmas there. "He does, actually. Like my own, they've elected to stay in London for the holiday."

Johnson pulled out a drab day gown and held it out for Katherine's approval. "It's nearly Christmas, Johnson. Let's go with something a bit more festive," she suggested, thinking she might mention having accepted an offer of marriage from the duke. Right now, it was a secret she wanted to hold onto for a few minutes more, though. Once the household knew, things would change around Whyte Hall Park.

Perhaps for the better.

"Of course, ma'am," the lady's maid said as she emerged from the dressing room with a pink day gown.

"That's better." Once she was wearing the gown, she regarded her reflection in the cheval mirror, happy to see her earlier appearance was still intact, the pink sprigged muslin enhancing her morning blush.

"You're certainly farther along in your morning ablutions than I expected you would be," Thomas said, appearing from the dressing room door. He bowed slightly.

Johnson gave a start, barely stifling a yelp of surprise. She dipped into a very deep curtsy as Katherine turned and did the same. When she straightened, she held out her hand. "I didn't wish to keep you waiting, Your Grace."

"You're very pretty in pink," he said, pulling on her outstretched hand until she was close enough for him to kiss her on the lips. "Good morning." He ignored the servant, but knew her eyes were wide with shock.

"I see you found some clothes. They seem to fit you rather well," Katherine remarked as her gaze drifted down the front of his body.

She couldn't remember ever seeing Whyte wear the silver embroidered waistcoat that winked above the buttons of the navy superfine topcoat Thomas was wearing. The matching navy pantaloons hugged his calves and were tucked into black shoes bearing silver buckles.

"They do indeed," he replied, his attention finally going to the servant.

Katherine held out her other hand. "Thomas, Duke of Pendleton, this is Johnson, my lady's maid," she said by way of introduction.

He nodded to the servant. "Mrs. Johnson. Thank you for seeing to my betrothed. I'll be escorting her downstairs now."

"Yes, Your Grace," Johnson replied, her eyes even wider than before. She dipped another curtsy and hurried from the bedchamber.

Turning to give him a quelling glance, Katherine said, "I hadn't yet told her of our plans."

He chuckled but quickly sobered. "She'll no doubt share them with everyone below stairs, so I dare not delay speaking with your driver any longer."

"I understand," she said, placing a hand on his proffered arm. They took their leave of the bedchamber and headed down the stairs.

Katherine thought it curious there were no servants visible on the first floor. When they reached the ground floor, the footman who was usually on duty in the hall was missing. "This is odd," she murmured.

"What is?"

"The servants. They all seem to be missing from their posts," she said.

"Could the unfortunate fate of my

driver be the reason?" he asked with a grimace.

She gave him a look of uncertainty. "They might be out in the stable, but..." She paused when she heard voices coming from the direction of the kitchen. "They could be having their breakfast."

Thomas led her down the hall toward the back of the house, his expression growing more serious. "I recognize one of those voices," he murmured.

"Well, I don't know how. I assure you, I haven't purloined anyone from your household," Katherine said when they paused in the doorway to discover the staff seated around a long trestle. At one end sat a man she didn't recognize, his hands clasped around a steaming mug of liquid.

"Well, I'll be damned," Thomas muttered.

She glanced up at him and blinked. "You look as if you've seen a ghost."

"That's because... because I'm looking at one," he whispered. In a louder voice, he said, "Fredericks? Is that you?"

The sound of the trestle's benches

scraping on the wood plank floor was accompanied by a round of gasps as all the servants stood and turned to stare. They belatedly bowed and curtsied in unison.

"Your Grace," Fredericks replied with excitement. "I can't tell you how relieved I am to see you didn't burn up in the fire."

Thomas blinked several times as he stepped into the kitchens. "How is it you're alive?" he asked in wonder, hurrying to join his driver at the head of the trestle. He clasped Frederick's shoulder and gave it a shake, as if he had to convince himself the man was real.

"I was just telling everyone here what happened," the driver said. "At least what I remember of it."

"When I found you in the snow... I was sure you were dead. I couldn't find a heartbeat. You weren't breathing," Thomas said in a quiet voice.

"Probably because I was half-frozen," the driver replied. "The 'orses woke me, which had me up and about real quick when I realized they wasn't hitched to the coach. Then I saw the flames. Didn't know it was the coach burning up until I was almost next to it. I can't tell you how fearful I was."

Thomas allowed a grin of relief before he furrowed his brows. "You spent the night out there?"

"I did, sir. But it was warm due to the fire. Found one of the coach lanterns and was able to relight it. Used it to find my valise and yours," he explained. "Your trunk broke loose from the back of the coach when it went into that ditch, so it didn't burn up, either. We brought it back in the coach Her Grace had sent to collect me," he added, his attention going to Katherine. "Much appreciated, Your Grace."

"I am so relieved you're well, Mr. Fredericks," she said. She approached and stood next to Thomas. "But didn't you have some sort of attack? Apoplexy?"

Fredericks grimaced before he bowed. "I did, Your Grace, but I think it was just something I ate at the last coaching inn we stopped at, when the 'orses were changed. Gave me an awful pain right in my heart."

One of his hands fisted, and he pounded his chest.

"You weren't hurt when you fell from the coach?" she asked in awe.

Blinking, the driver seemed to think a moment before he said, "Well, the snow must have cushioned my fall, I suppose. I'm sore this mornin', but nothin's broke."

"Well, that's a relief," she said. She turned her attention to the other servants. "Good morning, everyone. I'd like to introduce you to His Grace, the Duke of Pendleton," she added. "He'll soon be master of Whyte Hall Park since I've once again accepted his offer of marriage."

Thomas grinned and nodded several times as the servants reacted in surprise. A quick glance at Johnson had him realizing that with the arrival of his driver, the lady's maid hadn't been able to share the news of their betrothal. "I didn't mean to interrupt your breakfast," he said. "Please, carry on, and when you've finished—"

"We'll be ready for ours in the breakfast parlor," Katherine interrupted. "But not until Mr. Fredericks has finished sharing his gossip from London."

Despite her comment, Jackson hurried over to her. "I saw to it coffee and tea are ready for you and His Grace, ma'am," he said in a quiet voice. "Cook set out rolls and ham. She'll have eggs ready for you shortly."

"Very good, Jackson." She threaded her arm around the duke's and angled her head toward the door.

Curious, Thomas led her out of the kitchens and down the hall. "What was that all about?" he asked, his relief at learning the fate of his driver making his steps light.

"This is the most excitement my servants have had in a very long time," she said in a quiet voice, nodding toward the door to the breakfast parlor on their right. "With the weather, they haven't had the opportunity to go to town. Even for church," she explained. "They are bored, and they can't start hanging the greens until the day of Christmas Eve, so your driver's arrival is a welcome diversion."

"Ah, I understand," he replied. "Perhaps I should be glad *I* am not the diversion."

She tittered. "You are for me."

Thomas pulled out a chair for her, his brows furrowing at hearing her comment.

Katherine didn't see his expression, though, for she hurried to the sideboard and poured him a cup of coffee and her a cup of tea. "A very welcome diversion," she said. She set the cups on the table and then returned to the sideboard to dish up a plate for him.

He waited until she returned to the table with her breakfast before he took the chair next to hers. "Is that all I am to you? A diversion?"

Although the query came out sounding like a tease, Katherine sobered and stared at him a moment. "Hardly," she whispered. "I cannot tell you how often I have thought of you over the years."

The comment seemed to appease him, and he turned his attention on his break-fast. "I suppose I could say the same about you."

She stirred milk into her tea. "Rather uncharitable thoughts, I suppose."

"I understand now why you married

Whyte. I cannot fault you for what you had to do," he replied.

Katherine sighed. "I have spent a good deal of time wondering what life might have been like had we married—"

"As we should have," he interrupted in a whisper.

"Wondering how many children we might have had after Jonathan—"

"I would have named him John, after my grandfather—"

"—and if one or two of them might have been a daughter?" When he didn't reply, she angled her head to one side. "What?"

"I would have named her after a Greek goddess."

"Which one?"

"Well, not Aphrodite, of course, but maybe Cassandra or Charity—"

"Oh, I like Cassandra."

"—and I would have had to send her to a nunnery," Thomas claimed.

"A nunnery?" A look of alarm crossed Katherine's face.

"Or we'd have to live out in the country

somewhere, certainly not in London," he went on, shaking his head.

"But why?"

He scoffed, as if she should know the reason. "To keep all those young bucks away from her."

Matching his scoff, she said, "*You* were once one of those young bucks."

"Exactly. I remember very clearly what I was doing every afternoon with you," he reminded her.

Katherine giggled and then took a sip of tea. "As do I. I remember it fondly. Frequently. Which is part of why I look forward to picking up where we left off."

"At the altar," he murmured. "But only *part* of the reason?" he prompted.

Inhaling softly, she leaned over and kissed him on the corner of his mouth. "Marrying you means I can be a duchess again."

"You already are," he countered.

"I am *dowager* duchess," she corrected with a grimace. "The worse possible position to have in the aristocracy."

He shrugged. "So... you see marrying me

as a means of securing another title, and probably the coronet that goes with it," he complained.

"Oh, I forgot about the coronet," she said with a grin, her eyes widening in delight. She quickly sobered, understanding his expression of hurt. "Actually, the real reason I wish to marry you is because... well, I love you, Thomas. I always have. Even when you left me at the altar, I couldn't... I couldn't hate you."

He stared at her in wonder for a moment before he swallowed. "Oh. Well. When you put it like that..." He cupped one of her cheeks and kissed her quite thoroughly. "I suppose I can tolerate being a diversion."

"Just don't be driving coaches at break-neck speeds in the middle of the night," she warned.

"Now why would I do that when I can be in bed, spending my nights with you?" he countered.

She tittered and took another sip of tea. "Why, indeed?"

EPILOGUE

*C*hristmas *Eve, Front Salon, Whyte Hall Park*

The scents of pine and citrus wafted past Katherine's nose, and she straightened from reading a letter to discover Thomas leaning against the door frame to the front salon. He wasn't wearing a top coat, and his sleeves were rolled up to his elbows. A folded paper dangled from one of his hands.

She stood and rushed to him, kissing him on the cheek. "You look as if you've been engaged in something industrious," she said, one brow arching in appreciation.

He shrugged. "I might have helped haul

a rather large log into the house," he replied. "I can't imagine it will be entirely burned by the end of the Twelve Days, though," he added. "The thing is huge."

"Barker always says that, too, but it will," she said before kissing him on the cheek.

"It's beginning to look rather festive out here," he said, turning his head slightly to indicate the hall. "I expected you would be in the middle of concocting an elaborate wreath or wrapping the bannisters in pine boughs, and instead I find you in here."

"I am going to do all that and make some bows, too, but a letter from Jonathan arrived this morning," she said with excitement. "He received my note about your proposal and writes that he and my youngest will be witnesses for our wedding. We're to expect the entire family before the new year."

Thomas grinned and held up his paper. "John and George will be arriving within the week," he announced. "I read it twice because... well, I find it rather odd that our impending nuptials are enough to convince them to leave London for a week or so."

Scoffing, Katherine set aside Jonathan's letter and stepped into her betrothed's hold. "Other than beautifully decorated shop windows in New Bond Street, there isn't much to recommend London in December," she said. "Who wants to see soot-covered snow and gray clouds when they can be in the country for white snow and blue skies and all the decorations of Christmas?"

He chuckled. "There's that. My concern is *how* they're going to get here."

She gave a start. "What do you mean?"

"If you'll recall, the Pendleton traveling coach burned up," he reminded her.

Only the day before, they had taken a ride to the crash site to appease Thomas' curiosity. He had been shocked to realize he had walked nearly five miles in search of a light that led to Whyte Hall Park the week before. Despite the freezing trek, his toes seemed to have survived with no damage.

"Although John assures me there is another on order, it will be months before Tilbury has a coach finished," he added, referring to the manufacturer.

"Oh, that," she said with a dismissive wave. "I told you, Jonathan is bringing the *entire* family."

Thomas aimed a questioning glance in her direction before he stepped back. "*All* of my sons are coming in the Whyte traveling coach?" he asked in disbelief, his voice kept to a whisper.

"And mine. It was my idea," she said with a nod. "Although I did mention there should be two drivers. For safety sake," she quickly added.

"You minx," he said as a grin split his face.

"Happy Christmas," she said before once again kissing him on the cheek.

"Happy Christmas, indeed," he murmured, capturing her lips with his.

By the time he had finished his gesture of appreciation, Katherine's lips were as red as the bows she later tied onto the staircase bannister.

AFTERWORD

Your Invitation!

Do you crave historical romance filled with passion and red hot chemistry?

Come join me and my author friends in the Facebook group, Historical Harlots, for exclusive giveaways, chats with amazing HistRom authors, raunchy shenanigans, and more! **https://www.facebook.com/groups/2102138599813601**

ABOUT THE AUTHOR

A self-described nerd and lover of science, Linda Rae spent many years as a published technical writer specializing in 3D graphics workstations, software and 3D animation (her movie credits include SHREK and SHREK 2). Mythology, immortality, and ancient Greece have been lifelong interests.

A fan of action-adventure movies, she can frequently be found at the local cinema. Although she no longer has any tropical fish, she does follow the San Jose Sharks. She makes her home in Cody, Wyoming.

For more information:
www.lindaraesande.com
Sign up for Linda Rae's newsletter:
Regency Romance with a Twist
For articles on research and travels, read
Linda's Rae blog:
Regency Romance with a Twist